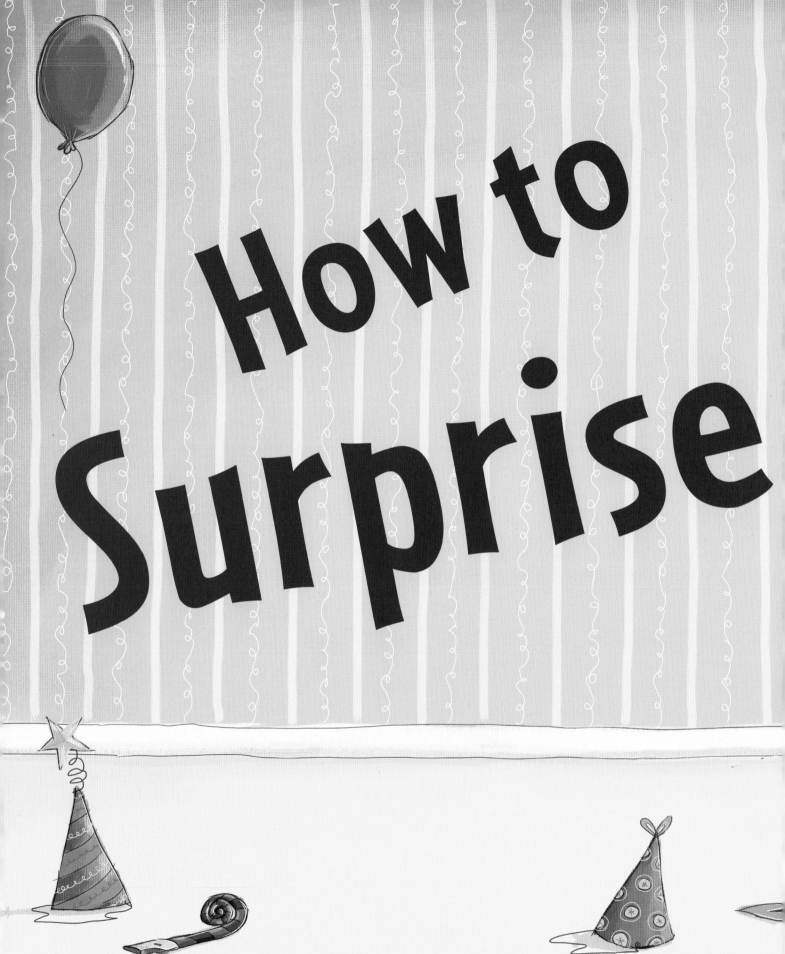

# How to Surprise

# a Dad

BY JEAN REAGAN    ILLUSTRATED BY LEE WILDISH

ALFRED A. KNOPF  NEW YORK

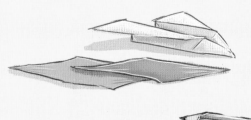

For John and Jane's dad
(SURPRISE!) —J.R.

Ivy, you surprise me all the time.
Love, Dad —L.W.

THIS IS A BORZOI BOOK PUBLISHED BY ALFRED A. KNOPF

Text copyright © 2015 by Jean Reagan
Jacket art and interior illustrations copyright © 2015 by Lee Wildish

All rights reserved. Published in the United States by Alfred A. Knopf, an imprint of Random House
Children's Books, a division of Random House LLC, a Penguin Random House Company, New York.

Knopf, Borzoi Books, and the colophon are registered trademarks of Random House LLC.

Visit us on the Web! randomhousekids.com
Educators and librarians, for a variety of teaching tools, visit us at RHTeachersLibrarians.com

Library of Congress Cataloging-in-Publication Data
Reagan, Jean.
How to surprise a dad / by Jean Reagan ; illustrated by Lee Wildish. — 1st ed.
pages   cm
Summary: "Two siblings provide instructions for how to surprise one's dad, including surprises you
can make, do, or find—and how to plan a Special Day surprise party for him." —Provided by publisher
ISBN 978-0-553-49836-3 (trade) — ISBN 978-0-553-49837-0 (lib. bdg.) — ISBN 978-0-553-49838-7 (ebook)
[1. Fathers—Fiction. 2. Surprise—Fiction.] I. Wildish, Lee, illustrator. II. Title.
PZ7.R2354Hr 2015
[E]—dc23
2014000563

The text of this book is set in 18-point Goudy Old Style.
The illustrations were created digitally.
MANUFACTURED IN CHINA
March 2015
10 9 8 7 6 5 4 3 2 1
First Edition

*Shhhhhhh!*
To surprise a dad, you have to be tricky.

First of all, don't let him
see this book.

HOW TO HIDE THIS BOOK:

Wrap it in paper and cover it
with pictures. (That way, he'll
never know it's about <u>him</u>.)

Tuck it between boring books no one ever reads.

Where's the Polka-Dotted Hippo book? *Wink, wink*

Make up a secret name for it, like—Polka-Dotted Hippo. (Be sure to wink when you say it.)

You may already be good at surprises, but do you want to become a *super dad surpriser*? Great!

Luckily, *any* day is a perfect day to surprise a dad, and there are so many different ways.

Some surprises, you MAKE:

Draw hearts and hide them everywhere.

Build a snow-dad.

Invent something amazing,
just for him.

Other surprises, you DO:

Get his toothbrush
ready.

Reorganize
his shoes
and hats.

Help him with the grocery shopping.

If you want to make him laugh, walk and talk like a dad.

Some surprises you don't *make* or *do*.
Instead, you . . .

. . . FIND them.

HOW TO FIND SURPRISES:

Look up, down, under, and all around.

Stay perfectly still and listen.

Dig a hole, sift through sand, or kick up leaves.

Kids have good eyes for nature (dads, not so much).
So surprise him when you find:

A caterpillar nibbling on a leaf. A squirrel hiding in a tree.
Dandelions for a bouquet. A heart-shaped rock.
A busy, busy anthill. Geese flying high above.

Now that you're an expert on *any* day surprises,
you are ready for . . . Special Day surprises!

These take a little more planning. (If your mom
is good at keeping secrets, ask her to help.)

SPECIAL DAYS FOR DADS:

His Birthday

Father's Day

Congratulations

Welcome Home

First, choose when to have the big surprise,
and decide who to invite:

Just your family?

Your pets?　　　Your stuffed animals?

His friends?　　　　　　　　Your friends?

Relatives?　　　　　　　　Neighbors?

Then, decorate with his favorite color. Keep it simple or go wild! (Remember to save some ideas for next time.)

Now, plan the yummiest part of the surprise—THE TREATS!

Create a dessert that looks like your dad.
Bake cookies with extra chocolate chips.

It's your dad's special day, so be sure to have his favorites:

Spicy chips
Smoked oysters
Super-stinky cheese

Don't forget presents!

PRESENTS FOR A DAD:

Shirt and tie.
(Instead of wrapping these,
<u>wear</u> them for an even
bigger surprise.)

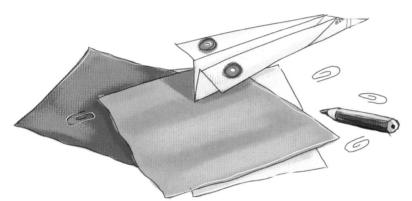

Everything you need
to make paper airplanes
together.

A secret treasure
map of your yard.

(Check also: ANY DAY SURPRISES you make, do, or find.)

If your dad gets suspicious and asks,

Look innocent.
(Practice this in a mirror.)

Say something like "Behind you,
it's very boring right now. You shouldn't
turn around."

Think fast—distract him with
a crazy dance!

When it's surprise time, make sure everyone is hiding.

HOW TO HIDE EVERYONE:

Between the pictures,
plants, or balloons.

*Surprise!*

Behind the curtains, couch, or coatrack.

Under the table, cushions, or blankets.

While you wait for your dad, practice whispering "Surprise!"

Okay, now *shhhhhhhh . . .*

Remember, of *all* the surprises, the best ones are
the special ones you dream up just for *your* dad.

Now, don't forget to hide this book. And *shhhhhhh!*

If you *do* want to let your dad read it,
have him say this pledge aloud
before he starts:

I, Dad,
promise not to remember
anything in this book.
Especially anything about surprises.

I ♥ DAD

✳ FOR DAD'S FAVORITE COOKIES
- flour
- chocolate
- eggs
- butter
- more chocolate
- sprinkles

DAD KEEP OUT!

ONE CLEAN ROOM COUPON.

Presents for DAD
- Drill
- Ball
- Hat and Scarf
- Hair gel
- Play day

LEAF FOR DAD

DAD + MOM = ME

TOP-SECRET!